Zack Rock

Homer Henry Hudson's Curio Museum

Creative & Editions

Everything has a story.

Take the Homer Henry Hudson Curio Museum. Looks like an old schoolhouse. And it did, once, serve the children of Bolshoi, four towns over. The Columbus Day Twisters of '67 sprang the schoolhouse skyward, where it leaped and pirouetted like a ballerina before landing here, upright, its dignified demeanor intact.

The museum houses—to quote one recklessly alliterative reviewer—"a colossal collection of curios, discovered, described, and displayed by that eccentric explorer extraordinaire: Homer Henry Hudson."

My job is to keep the place spick-and-span. My eyesight isn't what it used to be, but I'm a proper Magellan at nose navigation. You'd be surprised how well a 6th-century Byzantine bedpan keeps its distinctive aroma.

Lately, after closing shop, I've treated myself to a trek through the park and a sushi dinner. The walk exercises my feeble leg, and the fish diet helps maintain my dazzling figure. Chopsticks are a bother, but I'm confident I'll sort them out someday.

Everything has a story; the dullest clam may hold the brightest pearl. That's why each displayed artifact is accompanied by a description and a personal note from "that eccentric explorer extraordinaire" himself. When visitors float in, I sit quiet as a curio and let them follow their fancy around the exhibits.

Of course, there are a few favorite bits and bobs I silently hope they discover...

Item #: 0001

Name: Conatusaurus Skull
(Late Jurassic Period)

Location of Acquisition: Tigeham, Dorset,
England

Description: Skull of one of the smallest
dinosaurs to claw through prehistory. No bigger
than a chicken and as rubbish at flying: extensive
damage to the rest of the skeleton suggests it fell
to the earth after some ill-conceived takeoff.

H.H.H. Personal Note: My first discovery,
completely accidental. Found in the soil of my
family farm. This tiny skull planted in my mind
an unquenchable curiosity about the world: what
other treasures were out there, buried in dirt or
shadow, waiting to be brought to light?

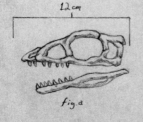
fig.a

fig.b

Item #: 0023

Name: Radial Tide Diviner

Location of Acquisition: Ionian Sea

Description: Device used by soothsayers on Calypso Island to predict the future based on tidal patterns. The island slipped below the sea after earthquakes struck in 487 B.C., taking the entire Calypsoian civilization with it. Shame the device never warned the soothsayers that their island sat on a massive fault line.

H.H.H. Personal Note: The discovery of the lost Calypsoian civilization during my years as a salvage worker around the Mediterranean Sea funded my career in exploration. While most of the artifacts were sold off, this I kept to remind me that the future is never set in stone (or, in this case, bronze).

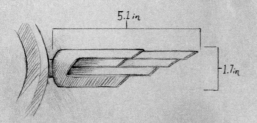

Item #: 1981

Name: Nóttlandian Stuffed Animal (bear)

Location of Acquisition: The Northern Kingdom of Nóttland

Description: Stuffed bear, knitted from hand-spun Arctic fox yarn. The Nóttlanders give newly shorn foxes wool sweaters to help them endure the northern winters. The wool-providing sheep are out of luck.

H.H.H. Personal Note: Gift from a young girl I plucked out of the rebels' grasp during the bloody Nóttlandian uprising. Delivered her to a country inn, miles from harm. She begged I accept her bear as a token of gratitude. Failed to get her name.

—8.3in

Item #: 3412

Name: Temple Montepaz Choir Finch

Location of Acquisition: Temple Montepaz,
Andes Mountain Range

Description: One of several finches taught to
chant different notes to accompany the temple's
parrot priest as he recites the traditional liturgy.
This specimen was a C#.

H.H.H. Personal Note: Reward from the temple's
caretakers for convincing the parrot priest to unbeak
a panel of wood he'd stripped off the dilapidated
temple wall. Closer inspection revealed the location
of a hidden city mapped across the panel's underside.
Kept that juicy morsel, and the panel, to myself.

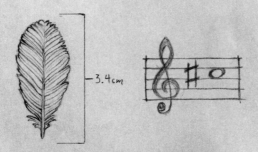

— 3.4cm

Item #: 3413

Name: Facade Fragment

Location of Acquisition: Unknown, South America

Description: Fragment of a colossal, ornate stone head. Significance unknown.

H.H.H. Personal Note: Once I snatched the map from the parrot priest, nothing could restrain me. I charged my plane toward the hidden city like a bull, blinded by the sparkle of imagined treasure. Though I lacked provisions, I rammed ahead. Though I flew through a porridge of fog, I rammed ahead. Then, I rammed a head. I crawled endless miles to find help, clutching this fragment.

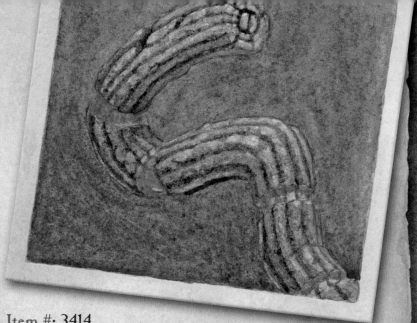

Item #: 3414

Name: Humble Willow Root Cane

Location of Acquisition: St. Francis Hospital,
Emerald City, WA, USA

Description: Walking cane fashioned from the
African Humble Willow tree root. The modest
plant can flourish only by bowing low enough
to sip the water of a nearby river through its
branches.

H.H.H. Personal Note: Given by my mechanic as I
recuperated from the plane crash. The cane's twisting
grooves echoed my inner anguish as I learned the
accident had forever impaired me. Each day, I would
laboriously hobble to the shore to watch airplanes
and boats bustle off to exotic locales without me.

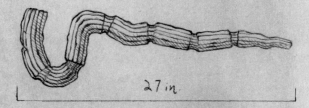

27 in.

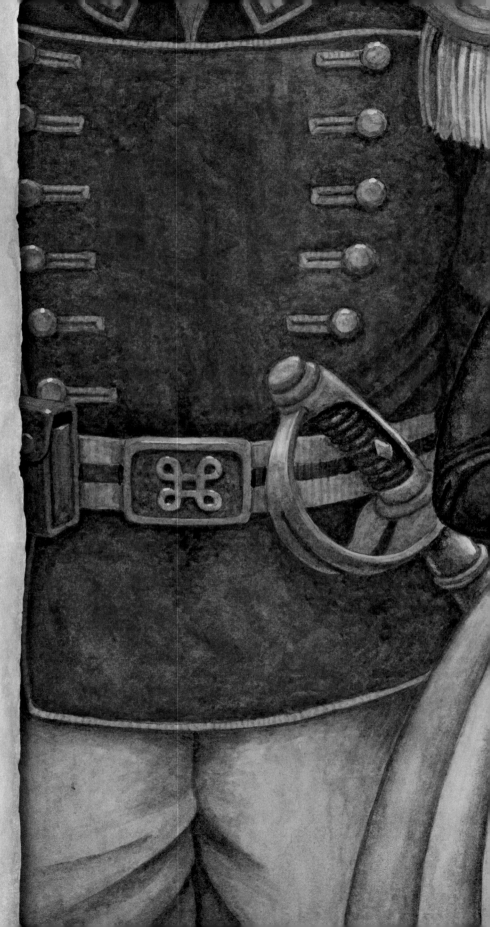

Item #: 3415

Name: The Manneken Mort of King Ingmar

Location of Acquisition: Homer Henry Hudson Curio Museum, Alexie Island, WA, USA

Description: Figurine composed of hundreds of thin fabric bands. When a Nóttlander passes away, their friends and family gather to tell stories about them. For each story, a bright new band is woven onto the figure.

H.H.H. Personal Note: To my astonishment, the little girl I rescued so many years ago knocked at the museum door one day holding the Manneken Mort of her father, King Ingmar of Nóttland. The king left me the figure as a parting gift for saving the life of his beloved daughter, Princess Bibi. Finally got her name.

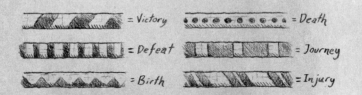

= Victory   = Death

= Defeat   = Journey

= Birth   = Injury

Of all the curios in the museum, I think of the Manneken Mort most often. I wonder, what would mine look like? Have the last of my bands been woven? Blimey, I've chewed on that question to the point of indigestion.

I'd like to think my Manneken Mort would be hundreds—thousands!—of feet tall. It'd tower over the Taj Mahal, shame the Sphinx! But I know few memorable tales are told of rusty old codgers who spent their days noshing fish and leaning upon fear like a crutch.

My luggage may be dusty. But my hat still fits.

Of course, I might meet with catastrophe. Swallowed in quicksand? Gnawed on by piranhas? Put down by a pox? Maybe. But there's no success without some failures. I have more than a few successes behind me.

Look around. Look closer.

That bit of cloud may be the first puff of a newborn volcano. Those tree bark scratches may be an obscure secret code. That discarded rock might once have been, or may someday be, the cornerstone of a great kingdom.

Everything has a story.

And mine isn't finished yet.

THE CURIO MUSEUM IS
CLOSED
UNTIL FURTHER NOTICE

Text and illustrations copyright © 2014 Zack Rock
Designed by Rita Marshall with Zack Rock
Published in 2014 by Creative Editions
P.O. Box 227, Mankato, MN 56002 USA
Creative Editions is an imprint of The Creative Company
Printed in Italy
Library of Congress Cataloging-in-Publication Data
Rock, Zack. Homer Henry Hudson's Curio Museum / by Zack Rock.
Summary: A knowledgeable canine caretaker introduces readers to an
exotic collection of museum treasures, becoming inspired to take
one last adventure of his own.
ISBN 978-1-56846-260-8
[1. Museums—Fiction. 2. Curiosities and wonders—Fiction.
3. Adventure and adventurers—Fiction. 4. Dogs—Fiction.] I. Title.
PZ7.R5883Hom 2014   [E]—dc23   2013041164
First Edition   9 8 7 6 5 4 3 2 1

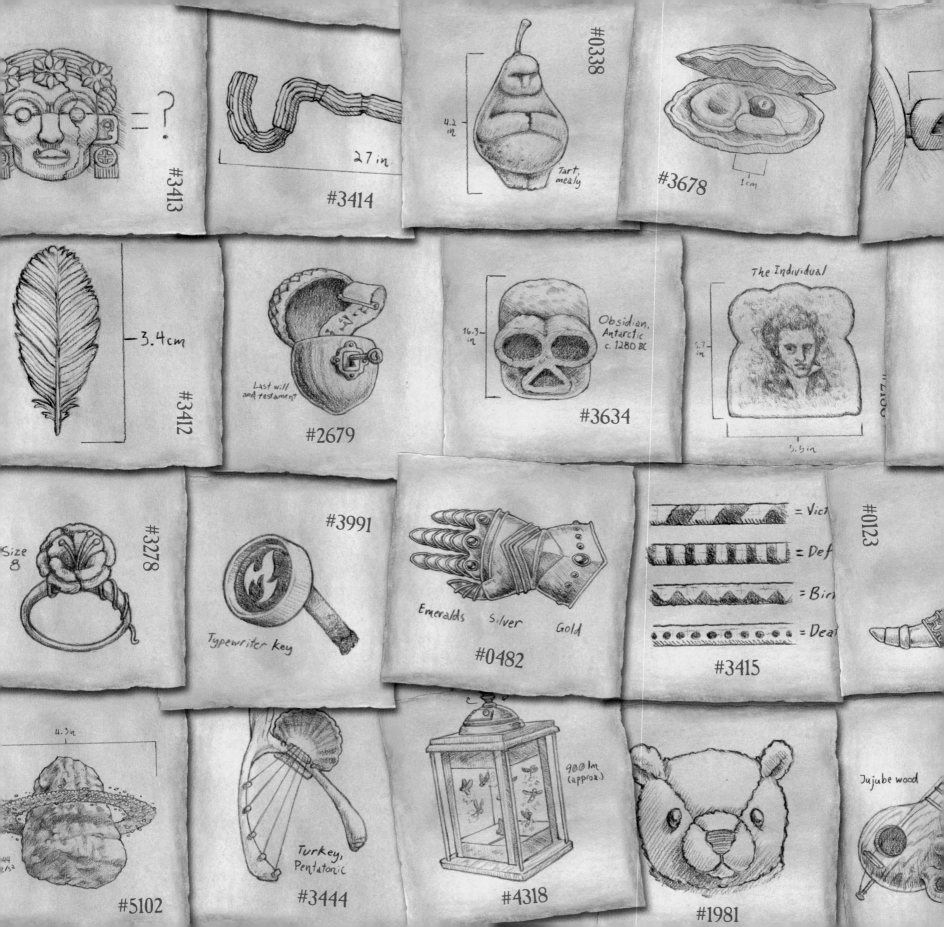

#3313

? =

#3414
27 in.

#0338
4.2 in
Tart, mealy

#3678
1 cm

3.4 cm
#3412

#2679
Last will and testament

#3634
16.3 in
Obsidian, Antarctic c. 1280 BC

The Individual
5.7 in
5.5 in

Size 8
#3278

#3991
Typewriter key

#0482
Emeralds   Silver   Gold

#0123
= Vict
= Def
= Bir
= Dea

#3415

4.3 in
#5102

Turkey, Pentatonic
#3444

#4318
900 lm (approx.)

#1981

Jujube wood